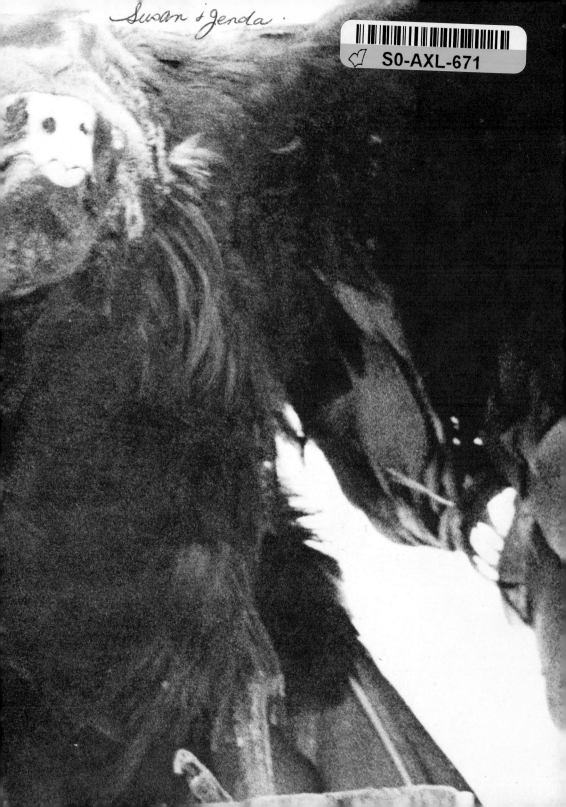

Susan & Jenda.

J. Power Buzzard

a
political
fable

**JOSEPH BENTI
and CAROL HENNING**

WOLLSTONECRAFT INCORPORATED, 9107 WILSHIRE BOULEVARD, BEVERLY HILLS, CA. 90210

Book Design by Ivy Bottini

PICTURE CREDITS

Shelly Cohen: *Title Page, 10, 12-13, 25, 44-45, 52-53, 63, 72, 89*

Susan Terry: *Front and Back End Sheets, 14, 18-19, 22-23, 30, 36-37, 40-41, 42-43, 48-49, 60-61, 68-69, 74-75, 77, 79, 80, 84, 91*

Wollstonecraft Incorporated
9107 Wilshire Boulevard
Beverly Hills, California 90210

ISBN 0-88381-002-6

Library of Congress Catalog Card Number: 73-82722

Manufactured in the United States of America

To A. Bella Buzzard and E. Walter Pigeon,
two birds who should live within us all.

The First Part

Was it morning, afternoon or dusk? One could not tell. Howling March winds whipped in from the west, sweeping giant swirls of dust across the bleak, granite plateaus and leaving a thick haze in their wake.

Here and there, a skeletal outcropping passing for a tree stretched up its blanched limbs in desperate supplication toward an unseen sky.

Peering through the dust, a solitary figure clung tenaciously to one of the barren branches. Its naked head

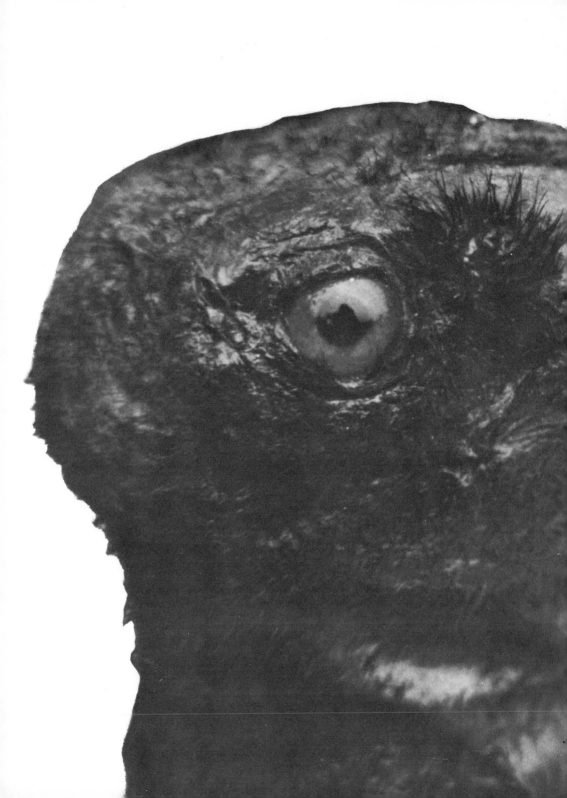

and neck of livid crimson slowly turned as it surveyed the eerie surroundings. Others might not be certain of the time of day, but here was one who knew precisely what time it was. This was J. Power Buzzard.

He knew that it was time for his flock to set out on a mission which would take them from their ignominious scavenging in this remote tip of Patagonia* to a new

* When the explorer Ferdinand Magellan first saw this land at the southernmost tip of the American continent, he noticed that the Indians living there had big feet. He named the area "Patagonia," which in Spanish, means "land of the big footed."

prosperity and an unchallenged place in avian history. If there was one thing J. Power respected, it was places in history.

For, J. Power was a turkey buzzard with a dream. Unlike the average *Cathartes aura*,* he knew the noble history of his kind. Indeed, almost 4,000 years ago, queens' crowns had borne the likeness of the vulture goddess Nekhbet, guardian deity of predynastic Upper Egypt.

Contemplation of these ancient glories stirred J. Power right down to the base of his feather bristles. And it was his will that all vultures, with his flock the vanguard, would reclaim the eminence once enjoyed by their ancestors.

Greatness would be theirs again. Long before he had taken over as flock leader, J. Power had hatched a staggering plan that was now his magnificent obsession, a plan he called "The Great Flight Forward."

Only his trusted adviser Henry Buzzinger, the bird who had taught J. Power all that thrilling history of the breed, knew of their flock leader's daring scheme to supplant the bald eagle as the national symbol of the United States of America.

An unusually strong gust of wind lashed the dust away from the lower part of the tree revealing three more

⌣

* Though commonly called turkey buzzards in the United States, *Cathartes aura* is neither a turkey nor a buzzard. It is a vulture. J. Power grudgingly accepts the bastardization of his species' name, but deplores such expressions as "that old buzzard."

figures, somewhat uneasy on their precarious perches. Squinting up at the leader were the aforementioned Henry and J. Power's fanatically loyal lieutenants, the Buzzarman twins.

B. B. and L. Ron Buzzarman had worked as carrion spotters until J. Power had plucked them from obscurity. They were the leader's lieutenants, technicians, and merciless executors of his slightest wish. Their dedication was so intense that they often carried out commands J. Power hadn't issued, but always in their leader's interest, or so they believed. The Buzzarmans' fierce devotion to J. Power was well known to the rest of the flock.

"I'd walk over my grandmother for J. Power Buzzard," L. Ron often said.

Henry never bothered with that kind of sycophantic devotion. He and J. Power had discovered each other at about the same time. In exchange for history lessons, Henry hooked his beak to a star and ascended with it.

Unlike the ascetic J. Power, who spent most evenings planning his great mission, Henry was seen more often than not waddling off to clandestine carrion suppers with his wing around a comely young buzzardess. Some old cynics wondered if he diddled as much as he dawdled. But Henry's reputation as flock flirt fit well into J. Power's scheme because it distracted attention from Buzzinger's vital role as policy maker and left the credit for all ideas to J. Power himself.

"The flock is nearly ready, JPB," hissed Henry as he looked up at the leader.

"I estimate we can be airborne in twenty-six minutes and nine seconds," added B. B.

"All systems are go," concluded L. Ron.

A steely determination crept into J. Power's eyes as he ruffled his Dracula cape of lustrous black feathers and unfolded his massive wings, one wing nearly catching in the crook of the tree.

"We are not going to Hinckley* this year," he announced. Only a turkey buzzard could have appreciated the shocking effect of that proclamation.

Henry had known all along of the change in destination, but B. B. and L. Ron were still reeling from the shock as J. Power continued.

"We are bypassing Hinckley to follow the path which will lead us to our rightful place in history. All the meetings we have held, the institution of confidence building classes, the periodic reviews Henry has presented of our noble past—all that was a prelude to this, our Great Flight Forward.

"It was no accident that We came to this flock. It was no accident that We were the youngest bird ever

---

* Hinckley, Ohio, is a town of about 5,000 inhabitants some 25 miles south of Cleveland. It has one claim to fame. Just as the swallows go back to San Juan Capistrano, the turkey buzzards return to Hinckley at the same time each spring. The only difference is that no one has written a hit song about them.

20

to win a perch on the Central Committee. We who travel the millenia, We who transcend those planes of existence which trap most others in the contented ignorance of being only where they find themselves, We are anything but accidental. We move beyond the limits of time and space to seize the opportunities for greatness and perfection.

"The time has come to restore respect to Buzzardhood. Those who endure the trials and the hardships of the journey ahead will show themselves worthy of the honors we claim not only for ourselves but for generations yet unborn."

As J. Power ended his speech, his majestic wings spread dramatically, nearly embracing the spellbound Buzzarmans and almost knocking Henry from his perch.

Deeply moved, B. B. swelled with pride and thought, "Surely he is the son of the Great One."

L. Ron fought back tears.

J. Power's eyes gleamed with a messianic fervor as he paused to note the impact of his words. Then he swiveled on his perch, looked out over the flock gathering below, and ordered his lieutenants to ready the flight formations.

The twins swooped from their branch, landing on a hillock in the midst of the milling flock. This was a time the birds anticipated each year, the journey from this barren place to the warmth of a unique and friendly welcome

from humans thousands of miles away. As yet the flock had not been told that this year would be different.

"The chief has issued the command to go north," the Buzzarmans declared to joyous snarls and hisses.* "He has made it clear that there will be no first night rest roost, and there will be only half the normal number of carrion calls."

Stunned silence greeted the directive. It was unprecedented, but the flock knew better than to question. Long ago they had learned that the Buzzarmans spoke for the leader, that they stood directly between J. Power and his followers, the better to screen him from any inappropriate ideas flock members might express. Every bird accepted this—every bird, that is, save A. Bella Buzzard.

She was a buzzard nobody pushed around, small and spirited with an unusually large, curved beak. "That pain in the crop," was the way the Buzzarmans generally referred to her.

Bella was the flock parliamentarian. Normally the job was ceremonial, but Bella had so mastered it that no flock Central Committee ever managed to circumvent her when she protested or raised a point of order. As evidence of her position, Bella had been elected two years in a row to represent the flock at the World Council of Vultures.

___

* Get used to the hissing and snarling now, because that's how turkey buzzards communicate. They cannot tweet, chirp, peep, honk, or caw. And, contrary to what some authors would have you believe, they do not talk either.

24

Now she lurched toward the Buzzarman brothers shrilling, "That's absurd! You can't take the young ones that distance without their normal rest and feeding."

"She's right," chimed in Shirley Buzzard, Bella's dearest friend.

"Even some of the adults will have trouble following that schedule. Why, Bernard's high blood pressure has been causing him to get dizzy spells just flying routine assignments."

Henry Buzzinger cut her off by addressing the flock in portentous tones. "Buzzards, we are about to embark on an historic mission which will take us far beyond this mundane existence of eating and sleeping. Just as our leader has said, 'We must dare to be great.' It is time to stop seeing ourselves as limited beings."

"Pinfeathers!" Bella shot back, but before she could continue, her mate, newly commissioned Wing Commander H. Bernard Buzzard, hopped forward.

"I can manage, Bella. I intend to prove worthy of my new assignment. I am ready to carry out the orders of our Commander in Chief. That is my duty."

There were loud snarls of approval from the flock. Bernard had expressed the feelings of the usually silent majority. J. Power's insistent portrayal of himself as the embodiment of Buzzarddom had worked. To criticize him was to betray the flock itself.

Bella emitted a frustrated hiss and stepped back

into the ranks. She knew how important it was to keep the flock united just before a major flight, and thus she subdued her inclination to force a confrontation now. She could wait until they were in Hinckley, until the young were settled down and the flock had recovered from its demanding journey.

"So much for Madame Big Beak," was B. B.'s smug hiss to his brother. "Our research team came up with a real zapper this time. Every bird's got a button, and hers is Bernard. I pushed it by hustling through that Wing Commander's commission for him. I know females, and you can bet next week's carrion that she won't do anything to screw up hubby's big chance."

Satisfied smirks blossomed on both beaks. With Bella silenced, the journey could begin.

At a sign from the leader, the twins turned and snarled the age-old flight command. "Flock off!"

One by one, squadrons flapped to the ready. Necks craned, and all eyes fixed upon J. Power Buzzard who pitched forward from his perch. Two wing flaps cleared him of the tree. He rose sharply, almost immediately catching the wind in his huge wings, and began to sail up through the dust. Wheeling in a magnificent arc, he nodded to those below.

Within seconds, the Patagonian sky was dark with ghoulishly majestic black shapes winging their way toward a rendezvous with destiny.

The Second Part

It was morning in Hinckley, Ohio. The recently deposited guano began to steam as the sun's first rays struck the roof of the combination town hall, library, post office and police and fire stations. E. Walter Pigeon paced the rain gutter, cooing plaintively.

Across the street at Bowman's General Store, townsfolk loitered listlessly, disappointment etched upon their drawn faces. Automobiles bearing license plates from Michigan, Indiana, and West Virginia turned their exhaust pipes on Hinckley and sped in disgust toward the distant lands whence they came.

Dejected birdwatchers, wasted and wan after a futile two week vigil, scanned the horizon through reddened eyes, binoculars dangling limply like carcasses about their necks. A park ranger, his face a mask of grief, wrung his hands helplessly as he eyed the vacant roosts at Hinckley Ridge and Whip's Ledge. The carrion he had so lovingly put out was going to the maggots. Nearby the children dawdled at their games, indifferent.

Hinckley's citizens were in the grip of this deep malaise because this year the turkey buzzards, annual harbingers of spring, had not come.

Long before there even was a Hinckley, about a dozen of the birds—advance guard of the eventual summer flock—had come to this place each spring. Their yearly arrival was recorded centuries ago in the tribal legend of the Wyandot Indians.

Usually the turkey buzzards showed up about March 15. Now it was the end of the month, and the weathered street banner, deserted booths in the school yard, and unsold commemorative sleeve patches only reminded the townsfolk that this year their Buzzard Festival, Hinckley's only big annual celebration, had been a fiasco.

It seemed as if Spring itself had boycotted Hinckley!

The local pigeons were taking the mysterious nonappearance even more seriously. After a long winter, these feathered citizens had come to see the buzzards' arrival as the surest sign of spring. It also meant a banquet of cake and cookie crumbs, half-eaten sandwiches, spilled popcorn, and, best of all, scraps from the big pancake and sausage breakfast in the Hinckley school cafeteria which, since 1957, had marked the beginning of Buzzard Day festivities.

Later that morning, the pigeons assembled on the town hall roof.

"Let the Palaver begin," declared counselor F. Lee Pigeon in sepulchral tones. Such conferences were called only in times of grave crisis, and just a few old timers remembered the last Palaver.

"As you all know, a situation of the utmost gravity brings us together. We have fallen on the hardest of times. Our once united flock is fragmenting in confusion and despair. At this very moment, some are even flying off to Cleveland and Cincinnati."

Gasps of disbelief escaped feathered throats. But some of the older birds knew why a few would weaken and emigrate to those two shining megalopolitan centers. Both cities' baseball fans are heralded throughout Pigeondom as the most generous in the major leagues. In 1970, Cleveland fans dropped nearly two tons of hot dog bun crumbs, popcorn and peanuts—a record for a regular season.

"We are losing members at an alarming rate," F. Lee Pigeon continued.

"If that is the will of the Great Pigeon," cooed N.

Vincent Pigeon, strutting to the Palaver Perch, "then, so be it. It is not for us to question."

"The Great Pigeon helps those who help themselves," a high-pitched voice answered back.

Young T. Fitzhugh Pigeon had never attended a Palaver before and did not realize the serious breach of etiquette he committed by exclaiming from the audience. Moreover, N. Vincent Pigeon was unused to being interrupted. He stared icily down his cere at the impetuous young bird.

Fitzhugh's confidence began to dissolve under a cacophony of derisive cooing. The crestfallen youngster was about to fly off in shame when the flock was addressed from on high.

"It will do us little good to begin attacking each other. We'd be much better off attacking the problem."

All eyes turned to find the source of the utterance. From his place of honor atop the town hall television antenna, E. Walter Pigeon had been following the proceedings. The flock fell into respectful silence as he ruffled his ancient feathers, strode confidently to the end of the antenna, and prepared to speak again.

E. Walter had served with distinction as a young bird in the nation's carrier corps during the Second World War. Furthermore, he believed that he was a direct descendant of Y. Mustafa Pigeon who carried messages for the Sultan of Baghdad during the twelfth century when the world's first pigeon post was established. His advice was seldom ignored.

"Our very presence here makes it obvious that we do not want to desert Hinckley. But our well being depends largely on the annual arrival of our avian cousins, and that is the problem. Perhaps they met with an accident or maybe they have been delayed by the elements. Their route of flight is known to all birds along the way; therefore, it seems to me that the most logical thing to do would be to fly that route in reverse and try to find the buzzards."

The wise old bird certainly made sense, but F. Lee summed up the reaction. "The trouble is, none of us is experienced enough. We've lived here all our lives, few of us ever travel. Why, even now we fear for the safety of those who recently left for the big cities."

The gray eminence of Hinckley's Birddom knew what he had to do. "I shall make the flight."

A chorus of happy cooing greeted his pledge.

E. Walter Pigeon spent the remainder of the day preening his feathers, limbering up his wings, and gathering a meager supply of stale bread crumbs, these he dropped into a tiny sack which he fastened to the ring around his left ankle.

At dawn, he set his beak in a determined line and flew off on what was to be the most important mission of his life.

The Third Part

Overhead soared dozens of turkey buzzards, their gaunt shapes casting deathly shadows on the green hills of French Lick, Indiana.* Others simply plopped unceremoniously on the ground, collapsing in exhaustion. The first birds to arrive had huddled against fence posts or had propped up their tired bodies in the crotches of trees.

In contrast to this forlorn scene, J. Power Buzzard

∨

* Honest, there really is a French Lick. It's in southern Indiana—near the Patoka River, northeast of Birdseye and southeast of Loogootee. Famous for its mineral water, French Lick has become a popular health resort and convention center.

invigorated despite the arduous flight, strutted trium-
phantly atop his command perch. This was another of
those historic moments that he loved to savor. He gazed
off into the distance as he hissed: "We have completed
Phase One of our mission. A small hop for a buzzard,
a giant swoop for Birdkind."

"Beautiful, Chief. A brilliant statement," B. B. remarked proudly. "That's the sort of thing that should be remembered for your history of the flock, Henry."

J. Power directed himself to his lieutenants. "We'll let the flock rest here as we prepare for the next and possibly the most crucial task ahead of us. I want reports from all wing commanders and roost captains within the half hour.

"Henry, I want you to leave for Vermilion* before dusk. B. B., you work out the details with him while I go buck up the flock with an inspirational word or two. I think I'll use that phrase about 'one small hop,' et cetera."

* Vermilion, Ohio, on the southern shore of Lake Erie, is about 40 miles northwest of Hinckley. Bald eagles nest there year after year, and it was with them that Henry would arrange a summit meeting that was to be the boldest diplomatic venture in the history of Birddom and the next phase in J. Power's Great Flight Forward.

As J. Power glided over to the bedraggled arrivals, the Buzzarmans took Henry aside.

"We have misgivings about leaving certain birds behind with the flock when we join you in Vermilion," B. B. confided. "It's possible that their sharp tongues and pernicious influence could dampen the enthusiasm of some of the less-committed flock members. We must protect the Chief from subversive elements."

"It would be, shall we say, beneficial to us all if these elements accompanied you and . . . uh . . . perhaps lost their bearings, as it were," added L. Ron.

Henry knew immediately what the Buzzarmans had in mind. It was a golden opportunity to get rid of two birds with one stone, so to speak.

Accompanied by two young buzzards of unquestioned loyalty Henry approached Bella and, knowing of her eagerness to get to Hinckley, convinced her that she and Shirley should join the advance party.

While Bella distrusted any of J. Power's lieutenants, she had no reason yet to suspect that Buzzinger, who somehow seemed above political intrigue, would resort to trickery.

Some of the flock wondered why Bella and Shirley would ever accompany J. Power's adviser on a mission, but others simply leered lasciviously at one another (as only buzzards can), assuming that Henry had hopes for an aviage à trois. As all knew, few females could resist his enigmatic charms.

Two days later, when J. Power, the Buzzarmans, a few young zealots, and H. Bernard Buzzard arrived in Vermilion, they found a supremely confident Henry awaiting them. Protocols had been prepared and an agreement in principle had been reached with the eagles. Henry had done his job well, and his quick, beady wink to the twins signaled that he had done his other job well also.

"It went off without a hitch," Henry confided behind his wing to B. B. and L. Ron. "Bella may be one helluva Parliamentarian, but she couldn't find her way around a carcass without a map. I lost them somewhere over Upper Sandusky."

For the moment, Bernard's concern over the whereabouts of Bella and Shirley was overshadowed by his sense of being involved in a world-shaking event. The meeting between the eagles and the buzzards was unprecedented in the annals of avian history.

The bald eagles were so imperious they never had extended recognition to other birds. This summit meeting was a testament to Henry's masterful diplomacy. He had convinced the proud eagles that the prospects for their survival would be improved by cooperating in an experimental project with the buzzards.

This was a crucial moment for J. Power. He must show the eagles that the agreement he wanted was in their best interests.

"Let us hope," he began, perching opposite the

head eagle, "that this joining of wings by our two great flocks will be an example to all Birdkind. We have much to offer each other. Our major accomplishment has been to proliferate—as you know, our numbers have not diminished appreciably in generations. In this hemisphere, we range from Canada to Tierra del Fuego. And you, fearless-feathered brethren, stand alone as the most noble winged hunters.

"We come to you because we wish to be carrion eaters no longer. Indeed, what are scavengers but welfare loafers? For centuries we have subsisted on the scraps left us by others. The average carrion eater is like a child in the family. If he becomes dependent on these handouts, if he is pampered and catered to, he loses his self-respect and his dignity. He becomes a soft, spoiled, and, eventually, a very weak bird. That is why the time has come for us to relish the rigors of self-reliance.

"From this day forward, we will rise above such beggers as pigeons and sparrows—sluggards who disgrace the name of 'bird.' Thanks to your graciously allowing us to observe your hunting techniques, we will succeed.

"Your boldness, your strength, your cunning, yes, even your ruthlessness, are inspiring examples to us all. Oh, there are those who would call you thieves because you sometimes appropriate fish and game caught by other, lesser birds. But I do not call that stealing; I call it enterprise, and I call it commendable."

J. Power had reached the heights of his oratorical skill. Eagles and buzzards alike flapped their wings in praise. So effective was his speech, the eagles suggested that some of the buzzards accompany them on a hunting mission immediately.

Alone with his lieutenants, J. Power was exultant.

"We've done it!" he gloated, strutting back and forth.

"Great presentation, Chief. You were masterful."

"You had them eating off your wingtips, JPB."

As the Buzzarmans rhapsodized over his speech, J. Power began a transformation. His eyes narrowed to a slitty glare of ferocity; his shoulders hunched up while his head moved down toward them, and his toes gouged the perch. Had he been able to get his feet on some arrows and an olive branch, J. Power thought, he would have been the embodiment of the Great Seal.

Later that night, Vermilion's handful of bald eagles had difficulty sleeping. It was as though the night had a thousand eyes, or at least a dozen, all beady and intense.

They were the eyes of the young zealots who had been assigned by the Buzzarmans to conduct round-the-clock surveillance of the eagles. Each eagle habit was to be studied meticulously and reported fully to the Buzzarmans who had begun compiling dossiers which they were confident would lead ultimately to the demise of the eagles.

There was another troubled sleeper that night. It had been quite a day for H. Bernard Buzzard. What with his natural fear of eagles and his role as a witness to history, he was an overwrought bird. Bella would have been proud of him, though, he thought. Come to think of it, where was Bella? Where was Shirley?

The nocturnal stillness was broken by shrill cries. "Bella! Bella! Shirley! Where are you? Bella! Shirley! It's me, Bernard."

Finally, an anxious Bernard made the mistake of poking his beak into the sanctum sanctorum itself, the cave that had been requisitioned as J. Power's headquarters.

In a trice, his wings were pinned beneath the toes of the outraged Buzzarman brothers.

"What in the name of the Great Buzzard do you think you are doing? You can't come in here without an appointment," the Buzzarman twins snarled in unison.

"Where's Bella? Where's Shirley? I've looked all over, and I can't find them anywhere. I know they left French Lick with Henry. I want to know where they are."

B. B. tried to pacify the disturbed wing commander. "They are . . . um . . . they're on a mission."

L. Ron helped his brother. "They're on an important assignment. It's classified, so it cannot be discussed. Besides, the Chief is asleep. Go back to your roost now, and you'll be told all you need to know in the morning." L. Ron folded his wings with finality. "We'll have no further comments at this time."

A rustling sound from the interior of the cave signaled that the leader was no longer asleep.

"Are you satisfied now?" B. B. snarled under his breath at Bernard.

"Have we completed the surveillance program?" J. Power inquired as he waddled to the mouth of the cave.

"Most of it, Chief," L. Ron offered as he tried to block Bernard from the leader's view.

Bernard, meantime, was trying to get up the courage to ask J. Power about the missing buzzards, when the leader noticed him.

"Greetings, wing commander. I'm glad to see you here. You must be proud of the important part you are playing in our Great Flight Forward. I can assure you that when we have replaced the eagle as this nation's symbol,

you will find yourself singled out for special honors."

The Buzzarmans cringed. This was one of the reasons they had methodically placed themselves between the leader and the rest of the flock. They had, in effect, become the ultimate censors, knowing full well that if allowed to extemporize, J. Power was likely to stick his foot in his beak.

Bernard wrinkled his red forehead in a perplexed frown. Replace the eagles?

"Wait a minute, sir," he blurted out. "You didn't say anything to the eagles about replacing them. We asked them to help us so we could better ourselves. That's all. If we're planning to replace them, why, that sounds like a betrayal of their trust . . . a . . . a . . . conspiracy."

A ruffled J. Power quickly recovered. "Conspiracy is a harsh word, wing commander. Let me just say this. It should be obvious to you that I have access to certain information which, for security reasons, is not available to the average flock members. I would suggest that you not allow appearances to blind you to the deeper significance of our actions.

"Let me make one more thing perfectly clear. The noble ends we seek must inevitably necessitate certain means upon which destiny exerts her influence and which find their justification in the inexorable flow of history. These things, my dear wing commander, cannot be simply explained or understood."

J. Power flexed his wings in preparation for take off and looked intently at Bernard.

"Our duty now is to return to the flock and remold it into a new and proud image," he snarled sonorously, taking to the air.

The Buzzarmans exchanged meaningful glances as they moved to each side of the confused Bernard. The wing commander had become a problem. He could prove embarrassing to the leader. He knew too much and asked too many questions. His naive moralizing could upset the grand design. The Chief had to be protected at all costs.

"An anticipatory defensive reaction is not contra-indicated here," B. B. hissed to his brother.

In other words, Bernard's number was up.

Assuring Bernard that they would take him to Bella and Shirley now, the twins flew off with him and headed out over Lake Erie.

The Fourth Part

The gloom that had shrouded Hinckley these many days darkened into tragedy one morning when a sparrow arrived at the town hall with heartbreaking news for the pigeons.

An emergency Palaver was called to allow the tiny messenger to address an apprehensive flock.

N. Vincent Pigeon opened the Palaver on a note of the utmost solemnity, and introduced the little sparrow who told this sad tale:

"A cousin of mine who spent the winter in Elyria said that all the birds there were talking about a pigeon, who I have since learned was on a mission for this flock, one E. Walter Pigeon.

"It seems this pigeon had picked up an important piece of information in Elyria and was on his way north towards a place called Vermilion when he had an accident."

The deep sighs and anxious murmurs of the assembled birds indicated more eloquently than words their

mounting apprehension and anticipation of personal loss.

"It's the strangest story. This pigeon, . . . uh . . . E. Walter, was flying along a determined course when he had a collision and simply disappeared."

"A collision?" several pigeons asked incredulously. "But he was our best flier. He went through the war without a scratch. How could he just disappear? With what did he collide?"

"A turkey buzzard," the sparrow answered simply. "A what?!"

E. Walter Pigeon never knew what hit him. When he came to, he found himself imprisoned in a downy blackness.

Bella had seen the imminent collision, but too late. She allowed the shock of seeing the other bird in her path distort her configuration, and her wings no longer obeyed. She began to lose altitude and somersault out of control. The force of the air pushed the smaller bird beneath her left wing.

Careening toward the earth. Bella used every feather

to try to brake. That effort plus some heavy brush mini-
mized the impact when the two birds hit the ground.

Shirley landed immediately and fluttered to the side
of the nearly unconscious Bella. To her relief, her friend
seemed none the worse for the crash. However, she com-
plained of a strange lump under her left wing. When Shirley leaned over to examine the lump, it cooed faintly.

Struggling to her feet, Bella shook the wing and
out plopped a dazed old pigeon. A smile spread slowly
across its beak as it focused on Bella and Shirley.

"Whew," it exclaimed. "You don't know how glad I am to see you two. A minute ago I thought I was on my way to that Great Coop in the Sky. My name is E. Walter Pigeon, from Hinckley, Ohio, buzzard capital of the world."

Bella and Shirley broke into friendly smiles.

"Hinckley? Gosh, that's where we thought we were going when we ran into you."

E. Walter explained his mission and corrected the two buzzards. "Well, from what I've been able to find out, your flock isn't going to Hinckley. It's in Vermilion, and I was headed there to find out why when we had our little accident."

"What in the world are they doing in Vermilion?" Shirley hissed. "They're supposed to be in Hinckley."

"I don't know," E. Walter replied. "But I've heard rumors of a big summit meeting with the eagles."

"So that's why Henry disappeared so fast," Shirley mused. "All that funny flying, those crazy zig-zags over Upper Sandusky. It wasn't because Henry was looking for a good place to eat. He was trying to ditch us."

"Obviously, Mister High-and-Mighty, Son-of-the-Great-Buzzard and his pals have something up their feathers that we weren't supposed to know about. We'd better get to Vermilion."

"Right, Bella. If you ask me, something's rotten in the State of Ohio. And I don't mean carrion."

The Fifth Part

The residents of French Lick, Indiana, had never seen anything like it. The once peaceful outskirts of their historic resort town had been invaded by turkey buzzards apparently gone mad.

Rabbits and other small creatures were shocked to see turkey buzzards swooping down on them. They were used to seeing the buzzards clean up after other birds of prey, but this was too much.

The seeming lunacy had begun some days ago. After resting up from their demanding flight north, the flock had been anxious to get to Hinckley. Then a rumor had begun to circulate that they would not go there after all.

Thus they had gathered in hushed expectancy to await the address to the flock which J. Power had scheduled for the morning of his return from Vermilion.

At that moment when their anxiety had reached fever pitch, the leader swooped grandly onto his perch above the flock.

"Fellow buzzards," he began. "When we left our southern nesting grounds, we set out on a flight that will determine the future of our species. Because of the momentous nature of our mission, we must eschew Hinckley for a much more important destination, one which will be revealed to you when the time is right.

"You, my flock, are participants in a project so glorious, so daring, that a weaker species would never dream of attempting it.

"Royal blood courses through our veins. Yet, despite our distinguished past, we have had to suffer the ignominy heaped upon the carrion eater. Humans have shunned, even persecuted us. I need only remind you of the infamous Laureles Ranch Massacre, those black, black days of which Henry has told us.*

* In the winter of 1918–1919, 3,500 turkey buzzards were trapped inside a wire enclosure on the Laureles Ranch in Texas. After the door of the cage would shut on a group of the birds, a Mexican ranch hand was sent in with a club to beat the innocent buzzards to death and burn their bodies. The reason for this carnage was that the birds were suspected, wrongly, of spreading anthrax and other livestock diseases. Actually, their systems are so antiseptic that they help stop the spread of disease.

"My fellow buzzards, this must never happen again. And, today, I make a solemn pledge to you that it never will. Instead, I see a generation—nay, a millennium—of greatness for our children and our children's children. I see a day when every turkey buzzard will hop in dignity. I see a day when all birds will look to us as leaders of the avian world. I see a day when our likeness will grace the coins and top the flagpoles of this great land.

"For you see, my beloved flock, we are destined to become the national symbol of these United States."

The birds reeled under the impact of this historic pronouncement.

"There are those who will foolishly ask, 'What of the bald eagle?' But I say what *of* the bald eagle? That so-called king of birds—who made him king? The answer is, impressionable and misguided humans.

"In their frenzy to find a member of our avian brotherhood to be their national symbol, these blundering humans even ignored the sage advice of one of those they call their Founding Fathers who said, and I quote:

" 'I wish the bald eagle had not been chosen as the representative of our country; he is a bird of bad moral character.'

"These immortal words were quilled by none other than Benjamin Franklin, inventor of the bifocal lens.

"In short, such a bird lacks our resourcefulness and will to greatness."

At this, the flock went wild. Almost to a bird, they were galvinized into a proud and militant entity. Now, J. Power's plan to transform the buzzard's image could be translated into action.

At daily grooming inspections, each buzzard was expected to be as trim as possible. Beaks were polished until they shone, feathers trimmed and combed, toe nails regularly clipped, and mint leaves nibbled after each feeding to combat the legendary buzzard breath.*

The Buzzarmans supervised stick-nest building on craggy cliffs and the tops of tall trees. More used to nesting in rotting tree stumps and caves on the ground, many of the buzzards spent half their time trying to keep their eggs from rolling out of the precariously perched nests.

The most demanding part of the program was the daily preyer meetings in which the males were formed into hunting squadrons and ordered to attack various small animals.

While turkey buzzards are marvelous aerobatic performers, such practices as power diving, abrupt pullouts, and swooping down into water, are not part of their normal repertoire. Thus, basic training activities were rife with near disasters.

---

* Turkey buzzard halitosis is reputed to be unmatched in its vileness. In fact, their bad odors are often their best defenses. When frightened, they disgorge the contents of their stomachs, which contents are said to have a stench so terrible that would-be attackers run or fly away, fast.

Bald eagles eat many dishes, but their favorite is fish, and it was a sight to see the buzzards plunge down into a lake, grab a fish, and then avoid drowning. Several are alive today only because of immediate beak-to-beak resuscitation. Others would have plummeted to watery graves had not the Buzzard of Fortune smiled down upon them.

Over land, the story was no better. Many had wrenched necks and sprained wings from failing to coordinate their dives from the sky with the movement of their intended prey on the ground.

Even those who did arrive on target and made contact with their prey, lost the tussle that followed. One buzzard had been savaged by a rabbit—a nasty experience for a future national symbol. Another had suffered severe whiplash while trying to hold an unwilling snake in its beak.

The most frustrating injuries suffered by the buzzards were the dislocated and sometimes cracked beaks which frequently resulted when the birds attempted to bite into whatever prey they miraculously managed to catch.

These last mishaps occurred because the turkey buzzard has one of the weakest beaks of any of the *falconiformes* order. They are usually unable to rend a fresh carcass sufficiently and so must wait until other creatures rip it open or until an advanced state of decomposition

has set in. This explains one of the turkey buzzard's cherished beliefs—that good carrion, like fine wine, improves with age.

"This is the key to the entire project," J. Power insisted in a conference with his lieutenants. "We take a back seat to none in our mastery of aerobatics and soaring, but strength and the appearance of virility are the main reasons for the bald eagle's over-rated image."

"We've worked with flock members for hours, but some of them just cannot be turned into hunters so quickly," hissed B. B.

"There are even a few who now say that if the Great Buzzard had meant for us to hunt like the bald eagle He would have given us their wings, talons, steel-strong beaks, and killer instinct," added L. Ron.

"Bah!" snarled J. Power. "Anybody can be taught to kill if the cause is just, and, make no mistake about it, our cause is just."

Eyes flashing, he wobbled resolutely to the front of the last squadron scheduled for preyer meeting that day.

"Follow me, buzzards!" he commanded. Immediately he flapped into the air, caught a powerful thermal, and began soaring as the squadron took to the air behind him.

Upward they spiraled as they soared to two, three, four hundred feet before leveling off. There was no exaggeration in J. Power's claim for the buzzard's soaring ability. Their bodies were suspended like magnificent pendulums as their flattened wings formed dihedral angles, a configuration which gives them unmatched flying stability and grace. But that was not nearly good enough for the challenge now before them.

"Learn to pull in your neck and your wings as you dive to your target," J. Power advised. "We've shown you silhouettes of the eagles. We've repeatedly gone over their configuration in flight. Now put it to the test. Forget the size of your wings and the distance between your head and shoulders. Will them into new shapes. Pull them into your body. Use your wingtips for control."

At this point, he spotted a raccoon. The others watched in astonishment as he hurtled toward the earth in a power dive, his body a speeding projectile heading right to target.

As he approached the ground, he surprised them again. A normal turkey buzzard would have never been able to pull out of such a dive. J. Power exerted his strength. Flexing his wings to the breaking point, he slowed his descent, changed the angle of his approach, thrust his feet toward the startled raccoon, and grasped it in his toes. Then he swooped up, flapping his massive wings as he dropped the animal to the rest of the flock which had gathered on the ground to watch his amazing display of flying skill.

J. Power soared above the flock. They raised such a cheer to celebrate his accomplishment that he smiled benignly. They were his. He signaled the birds still aloft to come in, and he landed in the midst of the flock to a near-deafening reception. Obviously savoring the moment, he raised his wings in an awkward "V" sign.

"You see, on our Flight to Greatness, I will not ask you to do anything that I myself will not attempt." J. Power assured his flock. "There is nothing you cannot do if you break the chains of the thoughts that hold you back. We can be perfect, unlimited beings."

He had saved his most provocative news for the flock council which he now called to order.

Phase Three of the Great Flight Forward was planned for the Fourth of July, 1976, the two-hundredth anniversary of the United States of America. The flock would fly to Washington, D. C., for a spectacular hover-in, the most impressive aerial demonstration in history. Buzzard delegations would be sent to circle every major city on the eastern seaboard. Of course it would follow that right thinking people all over the nation would demand that the turkey buzzard replace the bald eagle as national bird.

Nothing he had ever told the flock before could match this news. Hover over the White House? Perch on the great monuments? Stare down Senators and Congressmen, even the President himself? What genius! What an audacious move! J. Power basked in a triumphant glow. There were no limits now.

"Why stop there? Why don't you move into the White House while you're at it?" The sarcastic snarls of A. Bella Buzzard shattered his moment of supreme glory. He was furious. Where had *she* come from?

The Sixth Part

Bella's surprise return threatened to knock the Great
Flight Forward into a tailspin. The Buzzarmans moved pro-
tectively to their leader's side.

"I thought you said she was out of the way," he
muttered to the twins.

"There must have been a slip-up, Chief," B. B. replied.

"Henry said he'd taken care of her," L. Ron added.

J. Power glared at Bella and snarled angrily. "How
dare you interrupt a flock council! When you deserted
this flock, you gave up all your rights and your position."

"Shirley and I didn't desert the flock. We were led astray by that feathered Lothario who passes as your adviser. And we're not the only ones who have been deceived. Have you told the flock how you double-crossed the eagles?"

"Who cares about the eagles?" interjected some of the young zealots. "They'll soon be extinct anyway. Go back to your nest if you can't keep silent."

Shirley snarled, "Not until you hear about the double dealing and lying that has been committed in your name."

Bella knew the showdown had come. "What we have to tell you will reveal corruption in the highest councils of this flock."

L. Ron interrupted her. "Nonsense. Pay no attention to this shabby gossip. We will not dignify with comment stories based on hearsay, innuendo, or character assassination."

"Why don't you let the flock members decide what they want to hear," Shirley offered.

J. Power was grinding his beak in a rage. "The flock spoke clearly when it elected me leader by the most overwhelming majority ever. It is following me on a course to nobility and prosperity. It will not be misled by a couple of scandalmongering females who are trying to defame and discredit those loyal buzzards who have aided me in the burden of leadership."

"Listen," Bella addressed the flock. "Not only did these intriguers deceive the eagles, but one of our own flock was a victim of their treachery. I can prove it."

"This is slander of the most blatant stripe!" shouted B. B.

The Buzzarmans moved menacingly toward Bella.

Then, from out of nowhere it seemed, H. Bernard Buzzard swooped to the side of his mate. "If you so much as lay a pinfeather on her, I'll break your beaks!"

The twins were horror stricken. It was as if the wing commander had risen from the dead.

Pointing an accusing wing at the brothers, Bernard screamed. "I accuse these two of attempted avicide!"

There was a sharp intake of breath from the flock. For his part, J. Power was dumbfounded. He had known nothing of such a plot. Apparently, the Buzzarmans' zeal had exceeded their judgment.

"After Henry sabotaged Bella and Shirley," Bernard revealed, "the Buzzarmans promised they would lead me to my mate. They flew me out over Lake Erie, knowing full well that my high blood pressure causes me to have dizzy spells. After leading me round and round in circles, they abandoned me, thinking I would fall into the water and drown. I nearly did. I owe my life to the eagles, the very birds they betrayed.

"Shirley and Bella found me in Vermilion two days ago, and we flew straight here to expose these criminals."

"What do you have to say to that?" Bella asked the twins.

"All previous statements are inoperative, and we are not going to answer any more questions on the subject, no matter how they are phrased," L. Ron replied emphatically.

The flock members, some of whom were near hysteria, mumbled in confusion. Could it possibly be true that corruption reached all the way to the leader's perch?

Then, J. Power addressed them in a snarl dripping with unction. "My fellow buzzards, I am appalled at the disclosure of this senseless action and shocked to learn that my most trusted aides have been implicated.

"Now, in one of the most agonizing decisions of my leadership, I am requesting the resignations of B. B. and L. Ron Buzzarman—two of the finest birds it has been my privilege to know.

"But it is essential that we not be so distracted by events such as these that we neglect vital work before this flock. Our Great Flight Forward is the only hope for millions of vultures the world over. Indeed, we are on the verge of a major diplomatic victory. One of the birds slandered here today, my most trusted adviser Henry Buzzinger, at this very moment is flying west to meet with one of the major flocks in northern California. When his mission is completed, those who have attacked him will snarl his praises. The success of his efforts will bring together, for the first time, flocks of our species who will join us in the great hover-in.

"These are crucial days that require a united flock with a single purpose. I know that you share that purpose with me. I ask the Great Buzzard to guide all of us in the decisive days to come."

During the speech, the Buzzarman twins had stolen quietly away.

Bella persisted. "But you can't absolve yourself of guilt merely by offering up the Buzzarmans and some high-flown rhetoric. Whether or not you knew about the plot against Bernard, the fanatical loyalty which you required from your lieutenants led to such abuses of power.

"No goal justifies the deception you've encouraged or your arrogant assumption that you alone know what's good for this flock."

J. Power felt his control slipping away. That big-beaked trouble maker. Just like a female. They had no vision—always harping on petty details and not seeing the Big Picture.

"Half of you have been crippled by the eagle lessons. Is having your picture on money worth all this?" Bella asked the assembled buzzards.

By this time, many had begun to wonder, and there were some answering cries of "No!"

"Ingrates," thought J. Power. He whispered something to a young member of his staff who fluttered quickly away. Then, suddenly, J. Power stooped, regarded the flock with downcast eyes and allowed his beak to quiver a bit. He donned a humble demeanor as one would a tattered sweater.

"Let me remind you that the finest steel has to go through the hottest fire," he began. "I've suffered setbacks before, but my dedication to this flock has sustained me. Oh, I've made sacrifices. I've spent sleepless nights planning the great goals I want to achieve for the Buzzardhood."

With a dramatic sweep of his wing, he announced, "Here come two who know of my devotion to this flock."

All eyes riveted upon the staff member who escorted a withered female buzzard to the leader's perch. The ancient bird could hardly hop, and he supported her by tucking his wings under hers and sort of trundling her along in front of him.

In his beak, the young buzzard clasped a slender thread which served as the leash for an infinitesimal creature.

J. Power introduced the wizened old bird as "Mom" and the tiny thing on the end of the leash as his pet maggot, "Spot."

Response from the flock was predictable—respectful sighs for the aged mother and affectionate oohs and ahs for buzzard's best friend. Bella winced. How could one fight such a virtuoso heartstring tugger?

"Yes, these two have witnessed my pride in the accomplishments of this flock and my resolve when I've had to make a decision that was unpopular but right. Mom and faithful Spot know of the carrion calls I've skipped and the social life I've rejected to carry on with the vital work of remolding each and every buzzard within the sound of my hiss into a paragon of national symbolhood.

"I sincerely believe that this is the greatest flock in Birddom. But, and make no mistake about this, without the Glorious Goals I have given you, this flock will be cast back upon the carrion heaps of Patagonia to languish in obscurity once again."

"Begging your pardon sir, but that's not true," came a deep-throated coo. Circling the flock was a small gray bird who came to light on Bella's head.

"Hello. I'm E. Walter Pigeon and I'm from Hinckley, Ohio, buzzard capital of the world."

Nostalgia engulfed the birds.

"So it has come to this," J. Power thought bitterly. It was a crushing blow—a puny pigeon, one of those welfare loafers, addressing his flock. He wished he could have the pigeon removed, but at this point he didn't dare try. The leader felt helpless in the face of this humiliation. Oh, where were L. Ron and B. B.? Without lieutenants and advisers to shield him from such confrontations, J. Power realized that his control of the flock was dwindling drastically.

E. Walter wanted to reassure the buzzards, and his eyes misted as he fondly recalled his great-aunt Martha.*

"I can tell you that you are not the only creatures who have suffered indignities and persecution. And I promise you that there is a place where you are loved and missed. Hinckley wants you to come home.

"There's nothing wrong with trying to be the best you can be, but by now you must see that you can pay a terrible price for trying to be something you are not, for ignoring the limits nature has imposed upon us all.

"Your role as nature's garbage disposers is indispensible to all living things. It may not be glorious, but it is essential."

The looks of acceptance on the flock members' faces convinced J. Power that it was time for him to move on. Assuming his best eagle pose, he waddled off to the edge of the stunned flock and tensed for take off.

"What I do now, I do for the good of this flock." He screwed his beak into a wistful smile. "Take care of Mom and Spot. I'm off for California."

He flapped his wings twice, then turned toward the flock once more, hissing, "As I leave, let me say this, you won't have J. Power Buzzard to flock around anymore."

* M. Martha Pigeon, last of America's passenger pigeons, died at age twenty-nine in the Cincinnati Zoological Gardens at 1:00 P.M. on September 1, 1914. Her stuffed remains reside in the National Museum, Washington, D.C. At one time, the birds, native to this continent, numbered in the billions. Now, thanks to man, they are extinct.

It was an overcast morning in Hinckley. It had been that way for weeks. Old timers said they'd never seen such a bleak spring.

Up at Whip's Ledge, Bill Straw, a member of the Cleveland Audubon Society, was making notes on some geese he'd just sighted.

A ray of sunshine broke through the clouds and glinted off his binoculars. When he looked up, he saw them.

The flock was coming back to Hinckley.

It was a beautiful sight, but one that mystified Bill Straw. A turkey buzzard with an unusually large beak was leading the formation, and riding on her back was a small gray pigeon.

Vultures of Concord

by Keith Power

It is a golden sunset on Lynwood Drive, a pleasant suburban neighborhood in Concord [California] and time for the final twittering of song birds from the stately eucalyptus trees.

Regrettably for this particular grove, the best the hulking, bald-headed creatures roosting there can produce is a fetid hiss.

Silhouetted like ghastly visions from a prospector's nightmare, some 50 turkey vultures peer ominously down at the children and dogs rolicking in the 1700 block of Lynwood. Only visitors glance nervously upwards. Residents can match baleful stare with baleful stare.

"They are carrion eaters, the last in a line of nature's scavengers and very important ecologically," said Mrs. Daniel Denning with admirable detachment. "However, their personal hygiene is not so good."

The Dennings have come to know a good deal about the habits of turkey vultures. Their backyard at 1773 Lynwood possesses three of the 100-foot eucalyptus trees that have become the favorite roosting places for the birds.

The Dennings' trees were havens for more conventional birds when the family moved into the house a year ago. It is only in recent months that the vultures have settled down in large numbers.

The vultures, some with wing spreads of up to five feet, wheel on air currents over the remaining open spaces of central Contra Costa county.

Messy eaters, the big black birds spill bits of carrion onto the tidy backyard and patio of the Dennings. There is also a steady bombardment of droppings.

"If I let the dog out in the back yard," Mrs. Denning said, "I have to clean off his back before he comes into the house."

Worrying about health problems, the Dennings have placed the rear of their property out-of-bounds for their two girls. Every day or so, the Dennings scrub the patio surface and windows.

The answer to the Denning problem would appear to be a few volleys from a shotgun or the felling of the trees, Neither is possible.

The vultures, a wide-ranging migratory species, are protected by a Mexican-American treaty. The trees, among the oldest and tallest in Concord, are protected by Concord's heritage law.

On the advice of wildlife authorites, the Dennings tried scaring the birds away with blasts from shotgun shell blanks. The vultures wheeled lethargically to nearby trees and shortly returned.

Perhaps, if all of the neighbors fired away at the same time, the birds would be permanently discouraged. But this raised the prospect of turning the quietude of Lynwood drive into Normandy Beach on D-Day.

Mrs. Denning said her remaining hope is that the civic authorities of Concord, moved by the plight of the bespattered neighborhood, will pay for the expensive job of cutting off the vultures' high roosting branches.

As it is, winter descends and the big black birds spend more and more time just hanging around overhead.